the Stone- cutter

a Japanese folk tale

adapted & illustrated by
Gerald McDermott

PUFFIN BOOKS

FOR MY MOTHER

The author wishes to thank Sidney Forman
for his contribution to the original script
of the film <u>The Stonecutter</u>

PUFFIN BOOKS
Published by the Penguin Group
Penguin Putnam Books for Young Readers,
345 Hudson Street, New York, New York 10014, U.S.A.
Penguin Books Ltd, 27 Wrights Lane, London W8 5TZ, England
Penguin Books Australia Ltd, Ringwood, Victoria, Australia
Penguin Books Canada Ltd, 10 Alcorn Avenue, Toronto, Ontario, Canada M4V 3B
Penguin Books (N.Z.) Ltd, 182-190 Wairau Road, Auckland 10, New Zealand
Penguin Books Ltd, Registered Offices: Harmondsworth, Middlesex, England

First published by The Viking Press 1975
Published in Puffin Books 1978
20   19   18   17   16

Library of Congress Cataloging in Publication Data
McDermott, Gerald.   The stonecutter.
   SUMMARY: A retelling of the Japanese tale of a
stonecutter's foolish longing for power.
   |1. Folklore—Japan| I. Title.
PZ8.1.M159St 1978 |E| 77-25935
ISBN 0 14 050.289 0

Printed in the United States of America

Set in Koronna Extrabold

the Stone-
cutter

Tasaku was a lowly
stonecutter. Each day
the sound of his hammer
and chisel rang out as he
chipped away at the foot
of the mountain. He hewed
the blocks of stone that
formed the great temples
and palaces.

He asked for nothing more
than to work each day,
and this pleased the spirit
who lived in the mountains.

One day, a prince went by. Soldiers preceded him, musicians and dancers followed him. He was clothed in beautiful silk robes, and his servants carried him aloft. Tasaku watched until the magnificent procession had passed out of sight.

Tasaku cut no more stone
and returned to his hut.
He envied the prince. He
looked up into the sky and
wished aloud that he might
have such great wealth.
Then he slept.

The spirit who lived in
the mountains heard him...

and that night
transformed the
stonecutter into
a prince.

Tasaku was overjoyed.
He lived in a palace and
wore robes of the finest silk.
Musicians played for him
and servants bowed low.
He commanded great armies
and ruled over the land.

Every afternoon Tasaku
walked in his garden.
He loved the fragrant
petals and graceful vines.
But the sun burned his
flowers. He knelt over
the withered blossoms
and saw the power of
the sun.

Tasaku wanted to be as powerful, so he asked the spirit who lived in the mountains to change him into the sun.

The spirit heard him.

Tasaku became the sun, and he was happy for a time. To show his power he burned the fields and parched the lands. The people begged for water.

Then a cloud came and
covered him, and the
bright rays of the sun
were obscured. Tasaku
then knew the cloud
was even more powerful
than the sun. He told
the spirit to change him
into a cloud.

The spirit heard him.

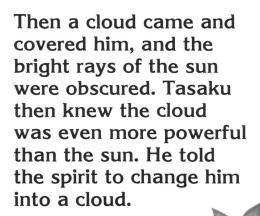

Tasaku became the cloud.
With his new power he made
violent storms. Thunder
rolled across the sky,
rivers overran their banks,
fields were flooded, huts
and palaces were washed
away.

But the mountain remained.

Tasaku was angry because
the mountain was more
powerful than the cloud.
"Make me into the mountain!"
Tasaku demanded. The
spirit obeyed and then
departed, for there was
nothing more he could do.

Tasaku became the mountain.
He was more powerful than
the prince, stronger than the
sun, mightier than the cloud.

But Tasaku felt the sharp sting of a chisel. It was a lowly stonecutter, chipping away at his feet.

Deep inside, he trembled.

ABOUT THE ARTIST

GERALD MCDERMOTT has created both animated films and
illustrated books. His graphic interpretation of mythology in
these media has brought him numerous international
awards. He recently had his first one-man show at the
Everson Museum in Syracuse and is now preparing a
limited edition of silk screen prints.

ABOUT THE BOOK

To prepare the art for this book, the artist hand colored
large sheets of white bond paper with gouache. He then cut
out his design forms and mounted them as collages. The art
was reproduced in four-color process. The text type is
Koronna Bold; the display is Serif Gothic Extra Bold.